ased on the "Winnie the Pooh" works by A.A. Milne and E.H. Shepard.

irst Edition
ibrary of Congress Cataloging-in-Publication Data on file.
ᴸBN 978-4231-3595-1

ˀ595-2325-7-11046

ᴹanufactured in the U.S.

ᶠor more Disney Press fun, visit www.disneybooks.com

DISNEY
Winnie the Pooh

Party in the Wood

By
Lisa Ann Marsoli

Illustrated by
Disney Storybook Artists

DISNEY PRESS
NEW YORK

It was a beautiful autumn morning in the
Hundred-Acre Wood—so beautiful, in fact, that
it made Winnie the Pooh feel like celebrating.

"All I need is a pot of honey," said Pooh,
"and friends to share it with."

Pooh set out to find his friends and happened upon Eeyore. Now, Eeyore was a rather glum sort of fellow. A party would be just the thing to cheer up the donkey.

"Eeyore," said Pooh, "how is it that you are at home, but your tail is not?"

"Isn't it?" answered Eeyore. "It must have fallen off while I was sleeping."

"I'll go see," offered Pooh. He crawled into Eeyore's house and searched high and low, but the tail was nowhere to be found.

"Could you check my backside again?" asked Eeyore. "In my experience, whenever my tail wanders off, it eventually wanders on again."

"I'm sorry," Pooh replied. "It's still not there."

"I can't say as I blame it," Eeyore admitted. "If I were a tail, I'd probably get tired of following me around, too."

"Well, we can't have a party until you have a tail," said Pooh. "Let's gather our friends. Together, we'll surely find a new tail for you."

Pooh went a few steps when he noticed a pinecone lying at his feet. Perhaps it would make a nice new tail for Eeyore. He picked up the pinecone and examined it closely from all sides.

"Too short . . . too sticky . . . too prickly for a tail," Pooh decided.

Pooh-koo!

Pooh went home to give the matter some more thought.
It was hard to concentrate, though, because his Pooh-koo
clock kept Pooh-koo-kooing! Suddenly, Pooh's little brain
had a rather big idea.

Pooh rushed back to Eeyore and found their friends had gathered around. He presented Eeyore with the Pooh-koo clock.

"Why thank you, Pooh," Eeyore remarked. Then he tried on his new tail, which everyone agreed was very becoming.

"Now we can celebrate!" declared Pooh. He was about to reach into a honeypot for a little smackerel . . .

CRUNCH!

. . . when suddenly, the clock let out a loud
POOH-KOO! It startled Eeyore, who toppled over—
and crushed the newest, noisiest part of himself.

"I think I fell back when I should have sprung forward," Eeyore explained.

"Well, if springing is what you want to do, why didn't you say so?" asked Tigger. He gave Eeyore tiggerific stripes and then attached a large coil to the donkey's backside.

"Hoo-hoo-hoo-hoo! Just follow me, Buddy
Boy!" Tigger said, bouncing away. But poor Eeyore
couldn't quite get the hang of it.

The search for Eeyore's tail continued.
"What about this?" asked Roo. He presented
Eeyore with a yo-yo. "You can make it do tricks!"

"Or not," said Eeyore.

Next, Piglet gave Eeyore a moose head.

Eeyore tried it on, but really couldn't make
heads or tails of it.

"Try this accordion," suggested Owl.

"I'm afraid I'm not very musical," Eeyore replied.

And when he tried to play his new tail, he
proved to everyone just how right he was.

Rabbit offered Eeyore a weather vane from his garden.
But as soon as it was attached, thunderclouds began to
form, and a lightning bolt struck the weather vane!

"Shocking," said Eeyore once the smoke had cleared.

"I have just the thing to replace your tail," said Kanga, pinning a
lovely knitted scarf to Eeyore's backside.

"Cozy," said the donkey approvingly.

"Honey time!" Pooh exclaimed.

But before Pooh could take even a taste, Eeyore caught the new tail
on a bush. The tail—and Pooh's party plans—quickly unraveled!

Eeyore looked more glum than ever.

"I have something that will lift your spirits," said Christopher Robin. He fastened a cheerful red balloon to the donkey.

"My spirits aren't the only thing it's lifting," Eeyore observed.

"Sorry, Eeyore," said Christopher Robin, removing the tail. "Let's see if we can find something more useful."

"Try my umbrella," Owl said. "I have found it to be very useful on many an inclement—that is, stormy—occasion. And you do seem to get rained on more than most, Eeyore."

"I guess I still will," replied Eeyore, since the umbrella ended up in exactly the wrong place to keep him dry.

By now, Pooh really was quite anxious to get to
the party part of the day—and he thought he knew
a way to move things along.

"Say 'hello' to your new tail, Eeyore!" he
exclaimed as he placed a party hat on Eeyore's rear.

"Sorry, Pooh," said Eeyore, "but I just don't think
my bottom ought to be happier than the rest of me."

"There are worse things than losing a tail,"
Eeyore said, "though I can't think of any right now."
He thanked his friends for their efforts and then
decided to return home.

Eeyore may have given up, but Pooh was more determined than ever to find a tail his friend would like. He wandered off and was looking high (after which he planned on looking low), when he spotted something that took his mind off of Eeyore's tail altogether.

Buzz Buzz Buzz Buzz

"Where there's bees, there's honey," said Pooh, thinking that his tail search would go much better with a tummy full of honey.

So Pooh reached inside the beehive. He felt the sweet, sticky honey inside the beehive. He heard a low BUZZZZZ.

BuzzzzzzzzZZZZZ

Then suddenly, a large swarm of bees poured out of the hive.

"Oh, bother," said Pooh as he took off running. And as he ran, he vowed that he would not be distracted from his tail search again.

Buzzzzzz

Pooh ran all the way to Owl's house, hoping that one of his
friend's many books might hold the solution to Eeyore's tail problem.

As Pooh rang the bell, he thought there was something awfully
familiar about Owl's bell rope.

"Come in, come in!" greeted Owl. "I see that you were admiring my new bell rope. Sit down and have some honey while I tell you the fascinating tale of how I came to find it."

Pooh listened as Owl described how he had found his newest prized possession stuck to a thistle bush.

"Owl," said Pooh, "I believe your new bell rope used to be—well, actually, still is—Eeyore's tail."

"Now that you mention it," replied Owl, "my bell has been sounding rather gloomy ever since I attached that rope. I mean, tail. Please return it to Eeyore with my best wishes, won't you Pooh?"

A short while later, Pooh delivered the tail to its
rightful owner.

Eeyore trotted in a circle, and the tail swung pleasantly from side
to side. The donkey breathed a sigh of relief. "Yup, that's my tail, all
right," he declared.

With Eeyore's tail troubles solved, Pooh gathered all their friends together again. "Party time at last!" he announced.

"I love parties!" cried Roo. "Are we celebrating finding Eeyore's tail?"

"Yes," replied Pooh. "That . . . and honey."

"And friendship," added Eeyore, remembering how very hard
everyone had tried to help him that day. "Friendship most of all."

J
Disney
(PIC)

Marsoli, Lisa
Party in the Wood